Rainbows

Written by
Anita Loughrey

Light is made up of seven colours:

red,

orange,

yellow,

green,

blue,

indigo

and violet.

You can use a triangle of glass to split white light into these colours.

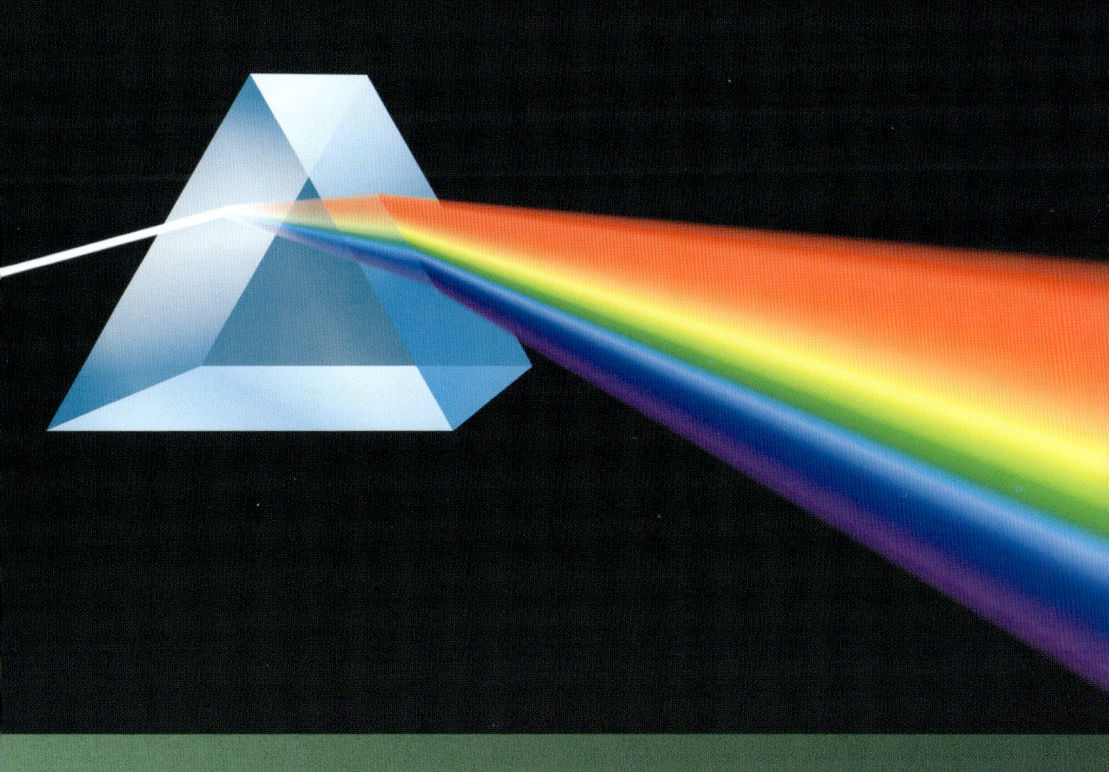

This glass triangle is called a **prism**.

A prism slows down the light.
It bends each colour in the light.

Each colour bends in a different way.

This makes a rainbow.

Raindrops are like little prisms.

Sunlight shines into the raindrops and the raindrops bend the sunlight.

This makes a rainbow.

You can see rainbows in many places. You can see rainbows in waterfalls.

You can see rainbows in fountains.

You can make rainbows at home.

You can see rainbows in sea spray.

You can see rainbows in bubbles.

You can see rainbows in shiny discs.
Pits in the disc bend the light.

You can see rainbows in oil from a car.

You can see rainbows at night.

The moonlight makes a rainbow in the rain.

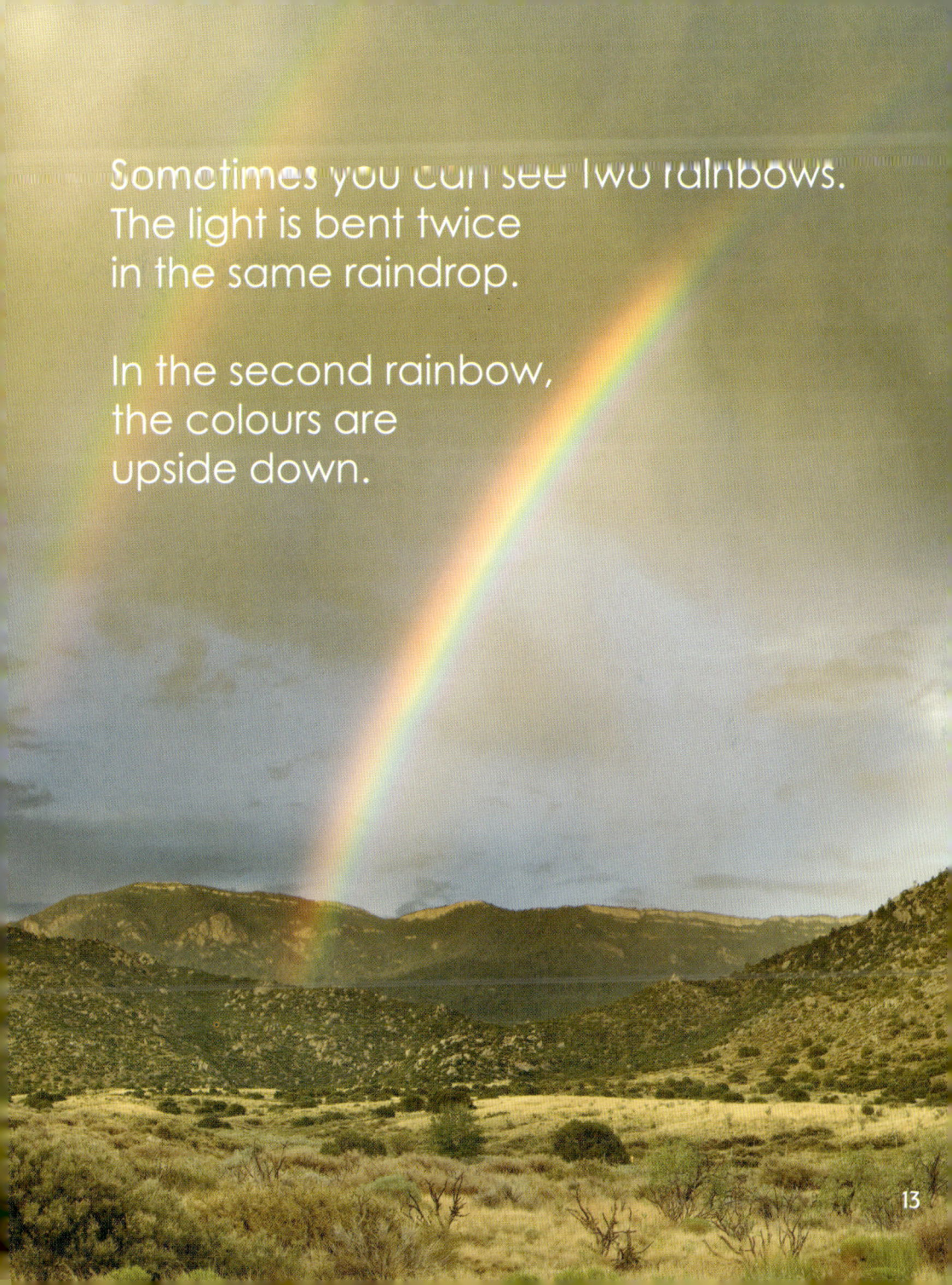

Sometimes you can see two rainbows.
The light is bent twice
in the same raindrop.

In the second rainbow,
the colours are
upside down.

Some people say you will find a pot of gold at the end of a rainbow.

It is very hard to find the end of a rainbow. When you move, the rainbow moves too.

Nobody has found gold yet!

Maybe you should keep looking.

Maybe one day you **will** find gold!